MESSAGE
ALERT
CU00855605

Titles in Between The Lines:

Badger Publishing Limited, Oldmedow Road, Hardwick Industrial Estate, King's Lynn PE30 4JJ

Telephone: 01438 791037

www.badgerlearning.co.uk

MESSAGE ALERT

ANN EVANS

Message Alert ISBN 978-1-78837-442-2

Text © Ann Evans 2019
Complete work © Badger Publishing Limited 2019

Publisher / Senior Editor: Danny Pearson
Editor: Claire Wood
Copyeditor: Cheryl Lanyon
Designer: Bigtop Design Ltd
Cover: © mooremedia/Shutterstock.com

4 6 8 10 9 7 5 3

CHAPTER 1

GOOD DAYS, BAD DAYS

"Mum! I'm home…"

I stop, key still in the lock. No smell of dinner cooking. No TV. Something isn't right. I just know it.

Dropping my school bag, I race through the house. "Mum!"

"Ellie…"

She sounds weak and my heart sinks. It hits rock bottom when I see her slumped on the kitchen floor. There's a puddle of tea and smashed crockery all around her.

"Oh, Mum!" I kneel and throw my arms around her. She's been crying, but her tears are dry now. "Did you fall?"

"My legs just gave way. I couldn't get up." She tries to smile. "Nothing new."

"How long have you been stuck here?"

Her eyes stray to the smashed mug and bowl. Her breakfast.

I feel like weeping. "All day! You've been stuck here all day? Why didn't you ring me?"

"Couldn't reach my phone." Her chin crumples. "I'm dying for the loo."

"Oh, Mum!" I hug her. This ME illness she suffers with is so unfair. It's a big mix of problems. There is no real treatment for it. It just saps all her energy and makes her body ache. She wasn't born with it. It came on after I was born. She got a bad infection and instead of getting better, she got slowly worse.

My dad must have seen the changes coming, so he cleared off before she needed too much help. I was three when he walked out on us.

I try to get Mum to her feet. She's not the lightest person in the world. We huff and puff — and even giggle as we struggle to get her onto a chair, and then the loo. Well, laughter is the best medicine! And Mum has never lost her sense of humour.

*

Once Mum is OK, we make dinner. I can peel vegetables much faster than her, but I let her think she's best at it. While dinner's cooking, I get the washing into the tumble dryer, run the vacuum around and tidy up.

"Any homework, Ellie?"

"A bit," I lie. I've actually got loads, but I'll do it later, once she's in bed.

I help her into bed at nine every night — except when she's having a good day. Ours is the ground floor of an apartment block, so no stairs, thankfully. By the time Mum's settled and my homework is done, it's gone eleven.

In our house we have good days and bad days.

The good days are when Mum isn't in any pain. Or when she's got a bit of energy and we can do things together. Good days are when we forget she's suffering from this horrible ME thing.

Bad days are when she's in so much pain that she cries. Or she's so tired she can't get out of bed. Bad days are when the ME completely takes over.

We have more bad days than good ones.

*

It's been such a busy evening, I'm in bed when I check my mobile. There's one message, from Janine. She'd sent it hours ago. We message each other most days. We have done for over a year now. We met online. I was reading up on ME and found a forum for teens whose parents suffer with it. Janine and I just sort of clicked.

We don't go on the forum now. We message each other privately on ChatApp. It helps to have a friend whose mum also suffers from ME.

Her dad didn't do a runner like mine, though.

My mates at school are sympathetic about my mum, but they don't really understand. And I don't want to go on about her all the time and bore them to death. So, Janine and I pour out our troubles to each other in private.

Hi Janine, sorry for late reply. Mum's had a bad day. How r u?

It's half an hour till her reply pings through, and I'm almost asleep.

I'm good. Mum's OK. We all went out for a pizza.

I feel a bit envious. It's been ages since Mum and I went out anywhere. I'm praying she'll be well enough for us to do something next weekend — my birthday.

I find a pizza emoji on my phone and send it saying, *Yum! Love pizza!*

She doesn't answer so I put my phone aside, tuck the duvet under my chin and sleep.

*

Mum's up and dressed next morning. Great — a good day!

"Mum, will you keep your phone in your pocket," I nag. "Call me if you're not well."

She gives me a hug as I put cereal into a bowl. "I'm feeling fine, Ellie. No dramas today."

We sit at the little kitchen table having breakfast together.

"What would you like to do for your birthday?"
she asks. "So long as… you know, I'm OK."

I remind her about my Saturday plans with my
mates from school. A movie and something to
eat. I'd kept Sunday — my actual birthday —
free, just in case Mum and I could go somewhere
together.

The bus stop is right outside our house, it's easy
to get into town or to the train station. My fingers
and toes are crossed!

"How about…" Mum says, "so long as I'm OK,
we get a coach to the theme park."

"Yes!" I squeal.

She laughs. "But I'm not going on any scary
rides, so don't even ask me."

"You'll have to watch me, then!"

I'm so happy, I run around the table and hug her.

"I've checked and I can hire a mobility scooter if I get tired."

"Yay! I'll get the L-plates!"

"Cheek!" she laughs, then adds, "You could bring a friend, but they would have to pay for themselves..."

I know our money situation. It's pretty tight. "No, it's fine. Let's just us two go. It'll be fun."

Her smile lights up her face.

I set off for school happy. Today is a good day.

If only I'd spotted the black clouds on the horizon...

CHAPTER 2
FRIENDS

My best friends at school are Katie and Jen. We spend first break chatting about which film we're going to see on Saturday. There are a few fit boys in our class, too. Katie says we should invite them along. I shrug. I don't mind — but I'm not doing the asking!

Katie goes right over and asks Tom and Bryn. She comes back grinning from ear to ear.

"Yep, they'll meet us there."

Jen pulls a face. "That's a bit uneven, two boys, three girls. Ellie, want me to ask Liam for you?"

I raise one eyebrow. "This isn't a date, we're not pairing up, are we?"

Katie puts on her dreamy face. "You never know."

Jen and I laugh. We all know Katie has fancied Tom for ages. I think she's using our trip out as an excuse. It doesn't matter. In fact, Liam is great. We get along OK.

He says yes, when Jen asks him. Then glances across at me and smiles.

I feel a bit shy suddenly and I look away to check my phone. Teachers know about my mum, so it's OK. I'm allowed to use my mobile at school.

Nothing from Mum, but I text her to check. She answers right back. *All good.*

I spot a ChatApp message from Janine. She'd sent it last night after I'd gone to sleep.

We should meet for a pizza one day.

"How's your mum?" I jump at the sound of Liam's voice. Then go a bit hot, as he's standing right there, smiling. Those deep brown eyes sparkling at me. "Thanks for the invite by the way."

"Katie and Jen's idea…" His face drops so I quickly add, "Sorry! I didn't mean it to sound like that. I'm glad you can come."

He shrugs. "No probs. So, it's your birthday on Saturday?"

"Sunday, actually…"

Jen and Katie link my arms, flashing wicked grins from me to Liam. They can be pretty silly at times.

"Not interrupting, are we?" Katie asks, mischievously.

"No, just talking about Saturday."

They both look at me like they've done me a huge favour, fixing me up with Liam. I blush, feeling so embarrassed. Liam just laughs.

He's cool about it. We all chat then, deciding what to see, and whether to have a burger first or pizza.

"What's happening on Sunday?" Liam asks me, after we've decided on burgers. "Your actual birthday?"

"Mum and I are going out for the day." It feels brilliant to say it and I cast the memory of her sprawled on the kitchen floor out of my mind. She would be fine for Sunday. She had to be!

"Where are you going?" asks Jen, her attention more on Bryn and Tom who had joined in the conversation.

"Theme park."

Katie squealed. "Love, love, love white-knuckle rides! We should all go in the holidays."

A hubbub of agreement springs up. They had all been before. Me, I've only seen it on TV and the internet. I'm not sure if I dare go on the really high, fast rides. My stomach fizzes at the very thought.

I text Mum again at lunchtime, just checking. She's good. She'd actually made it to the library. She loves reading. She's in lots of book groups online. She says she doesn't get lonely, she has so many online friends.

Janine had sent another message. *So, what do you think?*

About what, I wonder for a moment. Then remember her earlier message about meeting up for a pizza one day.

We've never actually met. That's the thing about online friends, they could be anywhere on Earth. Janine lives about 30 miles from me, so not the other side of the world.

We're the same age. Our birthdays are just a week apart. She has a younger brother, Sam, a dad who's a doctor, and a mum with the same illness mine has.

Janine could even spell it — Myalgic Encephalomyelitis.

No wonder they call it ME.

An afternoon of double English looms ahead so I quickly message back, *Yeah, brill!* Then I see Liam glance my way as I walk into class. My stomach fizzes again.

I can't wait for the weekend. It's going to be fantastic!

*

I smell spag bol the moment I turn the key. The TV is on and I hear pots clattering in the kitchen. My heart sings. Noisy and normal. A good day!

"Yum!" I say, tasting the rich, meaty mixture bubbling on the cooker.

Mum hugs me. "How was school?"

For some reason, Liam's smiling face jumps into my mind. "Good. There's a few of us going to the cinema on Saturday. We're going for a burger first."

"Sounds lovely."

"Have you been OK, Mum?"

She smiles at me but, just for a second, I see a worried look in her eye. My heart sinks. No, Mum, I think, please don't have a bad turn this weekend.

But she chats away about her day, asks me about mine. She's fine, I tell myself. She has to be. This weekend is so special.

We sit down to eat, but I see her arch her back, like it's hurting. I chat about the film, taking her mind off it. It's just a twinge.

I remind her about Sunday. "Have you booked the coach tickets, Mum?"

"Not yet, love. I'll do it on Saturday. Plenty of time."

At the last minute! In case we can't go. In case she's too poorly.

There's a lump in my throat.

"OK," I say brightly.

Disappointment is already setting in. Somehow, I look cheerful all through dinner. And all evening as we sit watching TV. But I can see she's in pain. She rubs her back when she thinks I'm not looking. She goes to bed early.

Alone, I pick up my phone. Click on ChatApp.

Janine, are you there?

I find the usual crying emoji and press Send.

CHAPTER 3

DON'T WORRY, BE HAPPY!

Maybe I'm worrying over nothing. Mum is up and dressed. We have breakfast and she waves me goodbye from the doorstep as I leave for school. She hasn't rubbed her back once.

"Keep your phone handy," I nag.

She taps her pocket.

It's Friday, and I'm sort of excited — but scared too. If Mum isn't well, all our plans will be ruined. And I really, really want to go out with Katie and

Jen… and Liam. And I really, really want to go with Mum to the theme park on Sunday.

If it doesn't happen, I'll be in bits. And Mum will hate herself for ruining my birthday. And I'll feel awful about that too.

"Oh!" I groan, and feel the tears stinging my eyes.

I rub them away, telling myself not to be so selfish. It's Mum who needs sympathy, not me!

My phone pings as I walk along. It's Janine. I open ChatApp and see our long line of messages from last night. Her mum had been poorly yesterday with a bad headache. So Janine was a bit upset too. We cheered each other up.

I re-read the last few messages.

Thanks, Ellie. Don't know what I'd do without you.

Nor me, I'd replied.

I read her latest message. *Morning, how's your mum?*

I tap my reply as I walk, saying she seems OK, but I'm so worried that this weekend won't happen. She says to keep my fingers crossed. Then says her mum is still in pain. Her dad is taking time off work.

There are no more messages from Janine. I guess she's reached her school, so I put my phone away.

I must look really miserable, as Liam is suddenly at my side saying, "Hey! Cheer up! Why the long face?"

"Oh, hi!"

He falls into step alongside me. "All set for the weekend?"

I do my best to smile. It doesn't work. And suddenly, all my worries blurt out on a flurry of tears.

"Aww, Ellie," he says, putting his arm around my shoulders. If I didn't feel so sad, it would be nice. "Listen, if your mum is ill and you can't do all the stuff you planned, it's not the end of the world. There's always other weekends."

I nod, feeling stupid. I blow my nose and it makes an embarrassing honking sound. I want the ground to open up and swallow me.

My phone pings again. I fumble for it.

"Your mum?" Liam asks, a worried look on his face.

"No. It's Janine."

He looks puzzled. "Who's Janine?"

"Oh, just an online friend. Her mum has ME too."

Liam nods. "Where did you meet her? At the hospital?"

"We haven't actually met," I say, deciding to read her message later. "We got chatting on an online forum. We've been friends for about a year."

"That's nice. Mutual support."

"Yes, exactly."

We reach school and Katie comes dashing over.

Liam spots his mates, pats my shoulder and heads off towards them. "See ya later," he says. "And keep smiling. It'll be OK."

*

But it wasn't OK. When I got home the house was silent. No dinner cooking. No TV. Mum wasn't slumped in the kitchen, thankfully. So I run into her bedroom — she's in bed, fast asleep. There are painkiller pills and a glass of water by her bed.

She looks so pale.

I know then that she won't have the energy to go to the theme park on Sunday. I don't wake her. I make dinner first, although I don't feel like eating.

My heart feels like a stone in my chest. I try my hardest not to cry. But I can't help it. My tears are falling silently down my cheeks, for Mum and for me.

With my eyes patted dry, I take her dinner through on a tray. She wakes sleepily as I sit on her bed.

"Oh, Ellie, I'm sorry. My back was hurting so much. I only meant to rest it for an hour."

I help her to sit up and we eat in her bedroom. She looks at me with such sad eyes. I know what's coming.

"Ellie, love, I don't think I'll be fit for Sunday."

"I know." I nod and put a bright smile on my face. "It's OK. Another time."

"I'm so sorry."

I hug her. "Honest, Mum. It's fine."

"You've got Saturday with your friends. Still go out. I'm fine on my own."

"You're sure?"

"Yes. And why not arrange to do something with them on Sunday?"

"But I don't like leaving you when you're not well."

She pats my hand. "I'll probably just sleep. See what you can sort out with Katie and Jen."

I smile. "OK."

I know I won't though. I'd feel foolish saying my birthday treat has been cancelled. I don't want their pity. I hold back the tears until I'm alone in my room.

*

Janine, are you there?

Hi Ellie, r u ok?

No. I add a crying emoji. *Mum not well. No theme park Sunday.* Another crying emoji.

Oh no!

And that's it. That's all she says. I sit and stare at my phone, waiting for her words of comfort and support.

Nothing.

A whole hour goes by and then my phone pings. I'm so relieved to see it's Janine. I don't know what I'd do without her to talk to.

Had a great idea. Had to check with Mum and Dad.

I send a puzzled emoji face.

*Come here Sunday. Having BBQ. Get train. Will
meet you at station.*

I read her message over and over. Meet up with
Janine! It seems unreal somehow. But inside my
stomach flips with excitement.

I'd love that! Smiling emoji.

For the rest of the evening we message back
and forth, making arrangements. I would catch
the 11am train and she, with her mum or dad,
would meet me at the station. Her parents have
even paid for my train ticket there and back.

It pings through on my phone.

At last, I'm going to meet my best online friend!

I can't wait!

CHAPTER 4
ARGUMENT

"You look lovely, Ellie!"

Mum is out of bed, but I'm sure she'll go back once I'm out.

I look at my reflection in the mirror. I've had this red top for ages, but Liam has never seen it. In fact, Liam has only ever seen me in my school uniform.

"Your hair looks beautiful," Mum goes on. "Love the way you've clipped it to one side."

"Thanks! I'd better go. Meeting Katie and Jen and a few others at 3pm."

She gives me a hug. "Have a wonderful time. And try to arrange something for tomorrow."

"Actually, I've been invited to a barbecue tomorrow," I say. Janine's name almost slips out of my mouth but I clamp it shut just in time. Mum doesn't know about Janine. I've never told her that I've needed someone to talk to. It would upset her too much.

"What, Ellie? You look like you were going to say something else."

"No, nothing," I shrug telling her not to worry, tomorrow's sorted.

"I'm sorry about the theme park."

"We can go another time, Mum. It's OK, really."

And it is. I can't wait to meet Janine.

*

"Here she comes! Here comes the birthday girl!"

Katie, Jen and the boys are all outside the cinema. I get hugs from everyone — even Liam. I can feel my cheeks glowing.

"For you!" Katie gives me a present. Jen does the same.

"Oh! Thank you!" I hug them both again.

"You can't open them till tomorrow!" Katie makes me promise.

As we head to the burger place, Liam says quietly, "I've got you something, too."

"You shouldn't have!" I say, as he places a tiny little doll made of cloth in my hand.

"Oh! It's so sweet!"

"It's a worry doll," he says. "From Asia. Every night, you tell the doll your worries. She hangs onto them and you get a good night's sleep."

I laugh. It's a nice idea.

"And," he adds, putting a piece of paper into my hand, "if that doesn't work, here's my phone number. You can tell me your worries — any time, day or night. I'm a good listener."

My eyes are stinging again.

Somehow, I try to say thank you without crying. But he grabs my hand and we run to catch the others up.

This is the best day ever!

Even though we pig out on cheeseburgers and fries, the boys buy big tubs of popcorn at the cinema. Liam sits by me, chatting, making me laugh. He's so lovely. It's a perfect afternoon.

*

Katie and Jen's bus arrives first. As they hop on, Katie shouts, "Have a brilliant day tomorrow!"

"I will! Bye. Thanks for the pressies!"

Tom and Bryn are walking home. Liam is standing here beside me.

"I'll wait with you till your bus comes."

I smile at him. "You don't have to…"

"I want to," he says, standing there looking at me. "So, your mum's OK for the theme park tomorrow?"

I tell him that she's not, but quickly add that it's fine, as I'm going to meet Janine and have a barbecue with her family. Oddly, he frowns.

"How are you getting there?"

I happily tell him. "11am train. Then Janine and her mum or dad will meet me. I guess we'll drive to her house."

"How will you know her?"

I groan, opening my phone. I've saved all the photos she's sent me. "This is her. That's her with her little brother, that's her at Christmas, that's her at the beach…"

"And your mum's OK with you going?"

"Well, I haven't actually told her about Janine. She knows I'm going to a barbecue…"

"But not that you're going on the train to meet some stranger. Someone you met on the internet! Ellie — think about it!"

"It's not like that!" I say. "Janine and I have known each other for ages."

"You don't know her at all," he argues. "Anyone could say they are a teenage girl and send photos they've downloaded."

My chest feels tight. He's got this all wrong. "Liam, she is real. We've talked so much over the last year."

"So, you have spoken to her?"

"Well not actually spoken, but messaged…"

He sighs as if I'm stupid. "Ellie, it could be anyone — a bloke."

"It's not!"

"Ring her then," he demands. "Call her now and let's hear her voice. Get her to put her mum on the line. Check this out."

"I will not!" I hate raising my voice. But he's doing everything to spoil my happiness. And I had really liked him. I'm glad to see my bus coming. "Anyway, here's my bus. Thank you for the doll."

I jump onboard and don't even look back at him.

His voice shouting "Ellie" rings in my ears all the way home.

CHAPTER 5

BIRTHDAY SURPRISES

I'm lying in bed, staring at my phone. I've added Liam's number to my contacts, but I don't suppose I'll ever ring him. I didn't give him my number. Not that I want to hear from him again.

Who does he think he is, telling me what I should and shouldn't do?

Does he really think I'm that foolish?

I feel awful. Really flat and sad. I message Janine. *Hi, can we talk? Really talk?*

There's no reply. Well, not till very late. The ping of her message wakes me. *Sorry, been out. Sooo looking forward to seeing you. Talk tomorrow!*

Putting my phone aside, my fingers touch the little worry doll. A beam of moonlight shines onto its face. "I am not worried about tomorrow!" I tell it sternly. Then softly add, "I'm a little bit worried about not telling my mum exactly where I'm going — it's just that I think she'll say what Liam said. But they're worrying over nothing. Janine is my friend."

I slip the doll under my pillow and sleep.

*

Mum is up, but I can tell she's putting on a brave face. Her back is hurting her.

"Happy birthday, Ellie!"

I open the card and presents. New jeans and a new top! Yes! Mum chose well, shopping online.

I open Katie and Jen's gifts then. Dangly earrings and a book by my favourite author. Brill!

I race upstairs and put all my new things on.

"What time will you be home?" Mum asks, as I'm about to set off.

"I'll be back by 8pm," I promise. I know, because my return train ticket says 7pm. Not that I can tell Mum about going on the train. She would only worry.

I've got butterflies in my stomach as I set off.

I take the bus into town, then walk to the train station. I'm early, so I message Janine.

I'm at the station! So excited!

I wait. And wait. And wait.

My train is due in one minute. I bring up her number and press Call. It rings out and then I hear a ping as her message comes through.

Hanging up, I read it just as my train pulls into the station.

Busy doing BBQ food. Meet you off the train.

Relieved, I step on board. Then have the biggest surprise of my life — Liam comes racing down the platform and hops onto the train. Breathless, he flops down beside me.

"Liam!"

The doors close and the train pulls off.

I stare and blink, and I know my mouth has dropped open in shock.

"Hi!" he says, and smiles.

"What are you doing here?" I ask him.

"Same as you, going to meet your friend Janine."

My head is spinning. "But you don't know her. She's my friend."

"You can never have too many friends. That's what I always say."

This is crazy. "But you're not invited. I can't just turn up with some random boy…"

That look is back in his eye. That worried look. "Chill! I'm not going to gate-crash the barbecue. Once I see Janine and her mum or dad — once I know she's for real — then I'll catch the first train home. And you'll never see me again. Well, you will, at school."

He's trying to make a joke of it but all I can do is blink. "Liam, this has nothing to do with you. You're not my dad!"

"No, I'm your mate, and I care about you."

His eyes burn right into me. And I know I should be glad that he cares. But I'm not a baby. I can make my own decisions. And I'm not stupid!

I can't believe that he's turned up like this. In one way I'm happy to see him. But he has no right to just turn up. I'm shocked into silence. We travel miles, not saying a word.

My phone pings. I read Janine's message. *In car with Mum. See you soon.*

Angrily, I shove my phone under Liam's nose. "See! I hope you like wasting your money on train tickets!"

He shrugs. "Money well spent."

I'm hot and flustered and glare at him. "I'll feel such a fool explaining you to Janine and her mum."

"I'll stay in the background," he shrugs. "Or say I just happened to be on the same train. There's no law against it."

Taking a deep breath, I order, "Stay in the background!"

"OK."

I ignore the hurt look on his face and turn away.
Silently, I watch fields and houses flashing by.
I feel awful inside. The flutter of excitement has
gone. Yesterday I really liked Liam. I still like him,
actually, but I'm so angry with him.

My phone pings. He glances at me as I read
the message.

*Disaster! Mum's car got a puncture. I've rung
Dad, he'll meet you at the station…* she goes
on to tell me what her dad looks like, and the
registration number of his car. *Make sure you
don't get into any stranger's car. See you at my
house. So excited to finally meet you!*

"What?" Liam asks, seeing the look on my face.

"Janine's mum's car has got a puncture, so it will
be her dad who picks me up."

Liam has gone very quiet. I know what
he's thinking.

"She expects you to get into some bloke's car? A guy you've never met? Ellie, you can't do this!"

"It's my friend's dad!" I almost shout.

"You hope! Ellie, I smell a rat."

"We are now arriving...," the announcer begins.

We're here. Liam doesn't move and I have to squeeze past him. Then he jumps up after me and follows me off the train.

"You're acting like a stalker!" I say angrily.

"Ellie, you cannot get into this man's car!"

His voice kind of shakes. Like he's really panicking. I storm off along the platform with Liam's warnings echoing in my ears. There are a few people about, waiting for their trains. Any one of the men could be Janine's dad. Tall with black hair. That's how she'd described him. What was I supposed to do? Go and ask them? That would be asking for trouble.

Janine's dad was looking out for a girl on her own. And Liam was like my shadow!

I slump down on a bench seat. Liam sits right next to me, looking over my shoulder as my fingers tap out a message to Janine.

At station. Is your dad here yet?

The moment I send it, a man standing just a few metres from me takes his mobile from his jacket pocket. He reads a message. Writes a message. Sends a message. Puts his mobile back in his pocket.

A second later my phone pings.

I glare at Liam, knowing he'd seen what I'd seen. "Coincidence! Everyone is on their phones."

I read Janine's message out loud. *Yes, should be. Think he's in a blue suit-jacket.*

"He's wearing a blue suit-jacket." Liam points at the man who just sent a message.

"Yes, but he won't have Janine's phone, will he!" I state. But then I start to get a sick feeling in my throat. With shaking fingers, I tap another message. *Can't see him.*

The man reaches into his pocket again. Reads a message. My message? Taps a reply.

My phone pings.

"Another coincidence?" Liam asks as I read.

I'm sure he'll spot you soon, Ellie.

"Ring Janine," Liam whispers.

My heart is pounding.

I call her.

Instantly, the phone rings in the man's pocket. My blood runs cold. Liam's arm slips around my shoulder as I start to tremble.

Liam and I watch the man standing just a few metres away. The tall, black-haired man, wearing a blue suit-jacket. He stares at his ringing phone. Then he cuts the ringing off and slips the mobile back into his pocket.

My phone stops calling.

I feel sick.

Liam holds me tight. I can't stop shaking. I think I'm really going to be sick.

"Pretend you're my girlfriend," Liam whispers, his arm tightly around my shoulder as we walk right past the man in the blue jacket.

Every nerve in my body tingles. I can even smell him. My legs feel weak.

Tricked.

I hate this man.

Janine never existed. I've been messaging this man for a year. I break free of Liam's arm and dash into the toilet to throw up.

Liam is right outside the door when I come out. His arm goes around me again.

"We need to tell someone," I breathe, glancing back at the man. He's tapping out a message.

My phone pings.

"Don't answer it," says Liam, as we head towards one of the station security men.

"OK, kids?" the security guard asks.

"Not really," says Liam. "Could we get the police here, please?"

*

They arrest the man who was sending me messages, the man pretending to be Janine.

Liam and I are sitting in a police car. There's a really nice police officer here. Three police officers bundle *him* into another police car. He's in handcuffs. Liam shields me as he looks our way. They drive off.

"Will I have to meet him?" I ask.

"No. We'll have his phone. We will need yours. Plenty of evidence to lock him away for a long time." She smiles. "Would you pair like a ride home?"

I nod.

"Ellie, I'll be coming in with you," the police officer says. "I need to speak to your parents."

"It's just my mum," I say as tears sting my eyes.

"Don't cry, Ellie," Liam says quietly as we're driven home by the police.

"This will break Mum's heart," I try to explain. "She'll be so hurt that I didn't talk to her about — well, everything."

"She'll understand," says Liam. "Trust me, mums always understand."

*

There's a birthday cake on the kitchen table.

"Ellie! You're home early. Look what I've…"
Mum's voice trails away as Liam and the police
officer follow me in.

She listens, drawing me closer as I tell her
everything. I knew she would be upset when I
told her I'd turned to an online stranger to tell my
troubles to, rather than her. But she hugs me.
Says that I can always talk to her — about the
ME, about my worries, or when I'm sad or upset.

I promise her that I will. I tell her I'm sorry for
being stupid.

She strokes my hair and says I'm not stupid, I'm
just too trusting. I'm not to blame. It's the cunning,
bad people of this world who are to blame.

The police officer says I'll need to make a
statement. But right now, I should enjoy the rest
of my birthday.

"Cake looks good!" Liam says, winking at me.

I get three plates and cut us all a slice.

"Happy birthday, Ellie," Liam says.

"Thank you, Liam. It's one I won't forget in a hurry."

Liam grins at me. "Understandable. You've been out with me!"

Mum and I laugh.

"Eat your cake!" I say.

THE END

ABOUT THE AUTHOR

Ann Evans lives in Coventry in the West Midlands. She has written over 30 books, including award-winning titles, *A Little Secret* and *The Beast*. She has worked on books for Badger Learning in their Teen Reads, Dark Reads and Between the Lines series. Ann also writes magazine articles on all kinds of topics.

Helplines and online support

Here are some excellent resources which can explain any difficult questions you might have:

www.nspcc.org.uk

www.youngminds.org.uk

www.childline.org.uk

www.actionforme.org.uk